Praise for

FIGHTERS

Fighters is a story about two sets of brothers on the Navajo Rez. All four are players of games—ordinary, everyday games like basketball, wrestling, and arm wrestling. When fighting, of course, one must look good and test limits. But when the brothers meet to play video games, a darker subtext is introduced by the mother of two of the boys. "You will be chased in your dreams," she warns. The boys walk past photos of the celebrated enlisted military fighters in the family to the bedroom where the game console is, where the game-fighters fight to the death. The brothers are curious to know more about why the older, defiant brother Jake spent the night in juvie. Moody, covered in nicks and cuts, Jake plays with a controller in one hand and a handgun in the other. The boys in this game-turned-dangerous keep testing limits while they are being delivered to an unexpected conclusion. It's all fun and games until it's not, and the reader is left spellbound by Chee Brossy's storytelling abilities.

—**CHARLENE TETERS**, a citizen of the Spokane Nation, is an artist, educator, and lecturer. Her paintings and art installations have been featured in over 21 major exhibitions, commissions, and collections.

More Praise

Fighters is a complex coming-of-age story set on the Navajo Reservation featuring two sets of brothers whose lives diverge and then converge again years later. Wyland, the young man at the center of these three connected stories, is trying to navigate the world of video games, competitive sports, girls, and a dangerous shadow world that exists just off-stage. In three books of poetry and now this novella, Chee Brossy has assembled a rich body of work that portrays the complexities, difficulties, and beauties of contemporary Navajo lives on and off the reservation. The work asks, among other questions: How does one go out into a fragmented, sometimes brutal, but also rich world of diverse cultures and retain one's ties to friends and family, language and culture, and ceremony? How does one walk in beauty in a world that often seems anything but beautiful?

—JON DAVIS, author of *Above the Bejeweled City* and *Nameless Now & Fearless*

FIGHTERS

FIGHTERS

A NOVELLA

CHEE BROSSY

★trp

TRP: The University Press of SHSU

Library of Congress Cataloging-in-Publication Data
Names: Brossy, Chee, author.
Title: Fighters : a novella / Chee Brossy.
Description: First edition. | Huntsville, Texas : TRP: The University Press of SHSU, 2025.
Identifiers: LCCN 2024047217 (print) | LCCN 2024047218 (ebook) | ISBN 9781680033984 (trade paperback) | ISBN 9781680033991 (ebook)
Subjects: LCGFT: Bildungsromans. | Novellas.
Classification: LCC PS3602.R6474 F54 2025 (print) | LCC PS3602.R6474 (ebook) | DDC 813/.6—dc23/eng/20241004
LC record available at https://lccn.loc.gov/2024047217
LC ebook record available at *https://lccn.loc.gov/2024047218*

FIRST EDITION

Cover photo by Stacy Brossy
Author photo by Teresa Montoya
Cover design by Cody Gates, Happenstance Type-O-Rama
Interior design by Maureen Forys, Happenstance Type-O-Rama

Printed and bound in the United States of America
First Edition Copyright: 2025

TRP: The University Press of SHSU
Huntsville, Texas 77341
texasreviewpress.org

★trp

for my family

CONTENTS

I

FIGHTERS

Cable was in eighth grade, a year older than my brother Lee, who was a year older than me. But Cable didn't make a big deal about it like my brother, who ignored me in the hallways at school and kept me out of basketball games with the older kids. I didn't like it, but I understood. You couldn't take shit. You couldn't be weak. Lee sometimes got into fights at school for slights I hardly noticed, maybe a guy staring at him funny in the hallway or whatever; he'd explode like a dog poked too many times. He always brushed me off when I asked him about the fights, like if I had to ask I just didn't get it. But I knew you had to protect your honor, your standing, because that was all you had.

Everyone on the rez played basketball, but Cable and his older brother Jake were wrestlers. The medals they'd won hung on their bedroom walls. Next to the medals was a framed photograph of Jake in a crouch—one leg in front of the other, hands ready, unsmiling, eyeing the camera, ready to leap onto his prey. The two of them reminded me of the leopards and lions I'd seen in a documentary at school. Every step they took was graceful, shoulders rolling under their fur, fast and sleek.

Lee had said once, and it stuck with me, "When Cable arm wrestles, his biceps are like potatoes." He said it matter-of-factly, and when Lee admired another boy's strength, I knew it was special. Even though I didn't sit with the seventh and eighth graders at lunch—and so didn't arm wrestle with them after we'd crushed our milk cartons with our fists and dumped our trays—I'd witnessed one of those battles. Jameson, an eighth grader with broad shoulders and a long thick braid had challenged Cable to an arm-wrestling match.

We'd been waiting every day to see it happen, could feel it coming in the way Cable didn't meet Jameson's eyes in the hallways, in the way he turned away and didn't laugh like the rest of us at Jameson's jokes. Cable just smiled his nervous smile with the dimple in his cheek. Jameson glared at his back, then started like he was going after Cable only to stop short at the last second and grin at us. Because Cable was the only one who was as big as Jameson, the only one who could match his arms and legs and neck.

The week before, at recess, Jameson got pissed at my best friend Roland for faking him out with a crossover. Jameson had been playing half-heartedly, toying with us and laughing, but then Roland, short and skinny, made a big show of his move, crowing on his way to the basket. Before Roland could shoot, Jameson caught him by the shoulders and the ball popped loose. Jameson grabbed Roland by the wrists and swung him around and around while Roland, screaming, scrabbled his feet on the court trying to gain traction, and then Jameson let him go. Roland's arms and legs were spread wide as flew. He stumbled and backpedaled over the shrubs at the edge of the court and landed with a thud and a yelp in the stickers.

Jameson turned, even the eighth graders were watching now; he smiled at all of us and raised his arms like the Ultimate Warrior. The bell rang and Jameson shouted, "Flawless victory!" the way they do in *Mortal Kombat*. Roland was his cousin.

When the coast was clear I ran over and helped Roland brush the stickers out of his jeans and T-shirt.

"That fucker," said Roland. His elbows were scraped up and he winced as he picked gravel out of his palm. "Why didn't you help me, man?"

I tried to pull him onto his feet but he slapped my hand away.

*

So when Jameson sat down across from Cable in the cafeteria, we all held our breath and leaned in. Even the lunch ladies in their tissue-paper hats stopped scraping the metal trays to watch. Jameson rolled his T-shirt sleeve up to his shoulder. I couldn't take my eyes off his giant bicep. He put his elbow on the table and squeezed his fist a few times like he was warming up.

With a nervous smile, as though to say, *alright, if we have to*, Cable reached out his own large hand and clasped Jameson's.

For a moment it looked like they were brothers, in a friendly contest. But then Roland shouted "Two-three-go!" and it was like two trucks smashing together.

The vein on Jameson's forehead stood out and so did the vein on Cable's neck, snaking down into his T-shirt collar.

Jameson grunted and growled, his eyebrows squeezed together, glaring at Cable.

Cable didn't meet Jameson's eyes but pushed air from the back of his throat through his clenched teeth, in a cross between a whine and a howl.

Roland reached in and pulled Cable's baggy T-shirt sleeve up off his arm. We all sucked in our breath. Cable's bicep was curved and flexed, bulging and pale, while the rest of his arm was brown.

Cable's face was turning red, and his arm began to shake.

Jameson bore down, shifting his feet and shoulders, pressing, lifting slightly off his seat and pushing Cable's arm past halfway down.

"Hey don't cheat!" someone yelled.

"Yeah!" someone answered.

The vein on his neck popping out like a rope, the back of his hand inches from the table, Cable caught Jameson's drive and held it there, his face a grimace of pain.

We were frozen too. We craned our necks, and girls had their hands over their mouths. Then something in Cable clicked.

The veins and the muscles still bulged, but now instead of Cable, instead of the pain in his face, the leopard was there.

It wasn't calm that drove those big animals and gave them their power, but desperation. Slowly, Cable turned Jameson back, inch by inch raising their hands, their fingernails white.

Then, reaching the midpoint, he gained momentum and twisted Jameson back into his seat. Jameson's eyes were squeezed shut, his teeth bared, his head trembling with the effort to stay alive.

With one final ragged breath, Cable slammed Jameson's hand onto the table.

It sounded like it hurt. Jameson grimaced.

Roland, still craning his neck, breathed, "Whoa."

Behind the kitchen sneeze-glass a metal pan clanged loudly to the floor.

Cable stood up shakily, his face still red, swung his leg to get out of the bench but caught his heel, and if he hadn't put out his hand he would've fallen on his face. He stumbled but stayed upright. He yanked his sleeve down, and, avoiding our eyes, walked out of the cafeteria.

The bus driver at the door didn't stop him.

Roland nodded and turned to all of us at the table. "Damn," he said. "He's *strong*."

Like a bell had sounded we all exploded out of our seats, running to the doors, shoving, jostling, shouting, trying to get to the basketball courts for what was left of lunch break.

*

Cable was a good guy—I liked that. He didn't trip kids in the halls or kick them in the nuts. I'd just learned about a kick to the balls. We were playing basketball at recess one day in the fall, and after sinking a game-winning jumpshot I yelled "Whatsup!" and pumped my fist. Keith Sagg who was part of Calvin's crew, walked right up and kicked me in the balls. It was like a live electric wire had been driven right up between my legs. The pain shot through my abdomen and sucked the breath from my lungs. I dropped to my knees on the concrete and curled over into a ball. The pain stayed there for a long time, shooting through my insides, making my legs weak. After I caught my breath, my eyes welled up and it took everything I had not to cry right there. Calvin pointed and laughed. The rest of his team laughed, too. I dragged myself to the edge of the court near the shrubs and tried to stand but I had to double over again. But really the worst part was the thud of the basketball, the shouts of Roland and the boys calling for a new game, running on like nothing had happened, like the world hadn't just been altered forever. I needed to start lifting weights.

But Cable wasn't very good at basketball. For all his strength he was awkward on the court, passed the ball, didn't want to dribble. Let other guys shoot, he said. But he still loved to play. He'd stand sheepishly on the sidelines until someone called his name. His eyes would light up. Then he'd run around the court like a wild man, smiling, leaping wantonly for rebounds, barreling us out of the way in his eagerness, mouth open, clutching the ball and letting out that hoarse whistle from the back of his throat when things got tight and the defense closed in.

I loved that he could have so much fun—I never laughed so hard as when I played with Cable. I forgot about the score and just ran and jumped, then ran and jumped some more, catching his same wild look, running after the ball and laughing until I couldn't stand straight and felt my ribs would burst.

With my brother it was different. I was tall for my age, but Lee was taller. When I tip-toed I was still shorter. Somehow Lee avoided the awkwardness of the other boys who grew fast, too fast for their own arms and legs to keep up when they ran, when they shot a basketball or threw a football. Our games were busting, bruising affairs from the first checked ball, and it was from him that I learned how to guard bigger players, how to stand my ground, to set my legs against a formidable, churning force. I had been bruised and beaten, and I'd cried during those lessons, but I learned them. I had also learned some tricks so I wouldn't be crushed flat every time. Lee would throw the ball at my head and I would check it at his nuts. We didn't throw punches—somehow that would mean that we weren't family, that we really had become enemies—but everything else was legal.

Lee's favorite move was to back me down with his butt, pounding the ball with measured dribbles, taking his time until he was under the basket, then turn and shoot right over my outstretched hand, rattling the chain net with his bank shot.

I told him once that he should learn a new move, that he was a boring basketball player. For a second Lee couldn't hide his hurt. We loved the game and devoted ourselves to it, wanted to honor it with our play, wanted to move like Jordan, like Barkley, like Pippen. We wanted to look good on the court. Looking good was as good as winning.

I was almost sorry I'd said it. Then Lee recovered, and the gleam came back in his eyes. Smirking, he said, "Why? This one works every time."

*

Cable learned everything he knew about wrestling from his brother Jake. I didn't know what wrestlers did because basketball shared the same season. But once at practice I'd gone to the water fountain the long way around to get an extra bit of air and peeked into Riggs' math classroom that doubled as the wrestling room after school.

The wrestlers were lined up on the floor lying side-by-side, the desks and everything cleared away, and Riggs was walking on their stomachs, stepping on guys extra hard so their air went out in a *whoof* and his foot sunk in and nearly touched the floor. "Come on," he was yelling, "what are you—girls?"

There was lots of groaning going on—and this was just the junior high team. Jake was in high school; I couldn't imagine the torture they put them through there.

I hadn't seen Jake in over a year. He was always away when we came by, out with the older guys driving his primer-gray Cutlass. Then it was like he disappeared altogether. Jake had a handsome face, slim bones in his cheeks. Up close he had pimples. I'd found out about acne that year, too, and soon I would be ducking into the bathroom between classes to see if my face looked okay, to pop pimples that I'd regret popping later.

The first memory that stands out in my mind of Jake is of him smoking a cigarette. It was evening and I was nine, playing tag with Tiara in the teacher housing park. We ran through the monkey bars and around the tractor tire, dragging our hands over its deep treads. Jake stood by the orange slide and inhaled, making the cigarette glow red, then blew out a cloud of smoke. He was thirteen, but he carried himself like a man. He watched us and smiled. More than the smoking it was his openness about it that stopped me running. He defied an authority that I'd never once thought of disobeying, and I felt dumb to be playing a kid's game.

Tiara caught up and slapped my arm, but I didn't move.

"Hey," she said, and pushed me. "You can't just stand there, you dork, that's against the rules." She was my age, the daughter of the junior high science teacher, and she didn't take crap.

I looked down at my hands. They were black with tire smudge. I wiped them on my pants where they left thick, dirty streaks. I looked up and Jake flicked his cigarette onto the slide. Tiara and I watched it trickle down the orange metal curve, leaving behind little red sparks until it landed in the dirt.

Tiara slapped my arm again, harder this time, and said, "You're it."

I told her I wasn't playing anymore.

Whenever I played tag after that, it was without the same fervor. I always had in the back of my mind an embarrassment—I was too old to be playing tag.

*

It was the end of June and shaping up to be a hot summer on the rez. Even the mornings were warm. By one o'clock it would be boiling and even the flies would quit buzzing and the dogs in the yards would find whatever sliver of shade they could and pant with their heads held just above their paws. It was a clear day, no clouds in the pale sky, and to the north, the Blanding Mountains, across the Utah border, looked closer than they were. On days like this it seemed that summer was too long. The streets of campus housing were empty, half of the teachers and school workers on vacation somewhere, our family's annual road trip to relatives in California was still a week away, and we seemed too far from everything. Too far from Farmington with its air-conditioned movie theaters and its mall with crowds and shoe stores, from the cool mountains, from Grandma's house an hour's drive away in Lukachukai with her open landscape of hills, rocks, and arroyos ripe for adventure, from our cousins' house ten miles beyond that. So when news reached Lee that Jake was coming back from a night in the juvenile center in Shiprock, he wanted to be there, and I didn't want to be left behind. I knew from the way Jess asked for more details that she wanted to go too, but being our little sister, she never got to come along.

It was Saturday morning when Lee announced he was going to Cable's to play video games. Mom told him to take me along.

Lee groaned.

"Why don't you boys play outside?" she said. "Video games are terrible, all that violence. Those things will give you bad dreams."

We had no game console at our house and, in fact, no TV. There was something about the bright colors of Mario Kart, or the never-ending quest to get past the ninjas with machine guns, the pixels that quivered with light and possibility that transfixed us. And then there was the best, greatest video game ever invented: *Mortal Kombat.* Just imagining the game made me daydream of a Nintendo of my own, where I could play constantly—studying, learning each character, all their special moves, their combos, their gruesome opponent-finishing *Fatalities*.

We'd go into Cable's room in the morning and come out as the sun was going down, and, after an entire Saturday of playing video games, hours hunched over the controller, my thumbs raw and tingling, I would unfold myself, breathe in the evening air, look over the fence that marked the boundary of our school neighborhood to see the late sun sinking beyond the Yazzie family house a mile away, fading red behind the distant buttes. I would stretch out my legs and back and feel a strange guilt. During all those hours in Cable's room the world had jumped ahead of me, and I would be a long time catching up.

I had been to Cable's house lots of times but still I savored everything: the thick, faintly moist air that smelled sometimes of laundry detergent, or on other days the delicious smell of frying bacon—something we didn't eat at our house. The dim interior was cut by bright streaking sunbeams that set the dust motes alight, thin maroon drapes over venetian blinds kept the light from glaring on the living room TV. The TV was always on, with Jheri-curled rappers cocking their heads, R&B singers crooning over their pianos in soft light, and Schwarzenegger saving the universe with his bulging biceps and a strangled wail. Carpet muffled footfalls in the living room; pebbled linoleum creaked in the hallway to the bedrooms in the back. And hung on the walls and propped on shelves all around were photos of every generation of enlisted Pashlakai: brothers, uncles, and cousins in Army helmets, Marine visors, and Navy caps. On one shelf a young Isaac, Cable's father, stood in a whitewashed archway with a pack strapped to his back, poised with his brown hands on each side of the arch, preparing to jump. He stared at the camera, not flinching or smiling—a soldier. Next to him was a faded black-and-white photo of a young man with smooth skin, a square jaw. It could have been Isaac's own father or uncle. In addition to his serious expression, he wore a Marine hat with a black plastic brim. There was a look in his eyes—some knowledge I didn't have—and often I found myself staring at him, trying to imagine what it was.

*

I stood behind Lee while he knocked on the trailer door. Cougar the pit bull boiled up their yard to the chain link fence that parallelled the road and kept him at bay—barking and gnashing his teeth. I flinched and raised my hand instinctively, but Lee stared him down. When Cable opened the door, he would let out a single "*Hey!*" and Cougar would stop barking and stare up at Cable curiously. But I still worried that Cougar would leap the low gate and sink his teeth into me. I'd been bitten in the leg by a neighborhood dog the summer before and now I tensed up around dogs.

The door opened with a sucking sound and behind it stood Cable's dad Isaac in shorts, barefoot. The smell of frying bacon swept over us.

Sometimes on a Saturday morning like this one Isaac would answer the door, look at us stoically, and then say gruffly over his shoulder, "Hey, it's them William boys." He dropped the 's' at the end of our name. Just his appearance sent Cougar slinking away.

"Say something in Navajo for me, boys." And we would say *Yá'át'ééh* for hello and that would loosen him up, shaking the crust from his face with a smile.

"Say 'Mud Man' for me."

"Mud Man," we'd say.

"No! In Navajo!" And he'd laugh.

And after a pause we'd say it, translating it literally as he'd asked, *Hashtł'ish hastįį*, and he'd laugh a deep belly laugh, tilting his head back, eyes squeezed shut behind his thick oval glasses. It had all the rhythm and stops, the air under the tongue and the sh-sounds that made it so unlike English. I thought it was funny that he wanted to hear us speak Navajo. I never thought it strange that we never heard him reply to us or ask us the questions in the language himself, though I was sure he spoke it fluently. But I did know that we were different, and that Isaac, like other people, loved that we were half-white, light-skinned boys who could speak.

But on other days Isaac was unsmiling when he opened the door, short with us, salted away somewhere behind his glasses. On those days *Mud Man* sounded strange, a tongue twister, harsh in its repetition, catching in our throats.

"Huh," Isaac said, looking down at us where we stood on the stairs, his hand still on the doorknob, his short dark hair pressed to his head on one side from sleep, wearing a wifebeater and old-school cotton gym shorts. I could hear the TV going in the living room. On his left hand he wore a metal watch that clinked when he adjusted his grip on the knob. We avoided him when he had his black uniform on, when he rode the streets of the neighborhood in his pickup with the lights on top and security shield on the door, the one that was parked in the space out front. He was thick-armed with knobby knuckles. His forearms were dark but his upper arms were pale, saved from the sun by the sleeves of his uniform.

Isaac walked away from the door, leaving it open. I leaned my head inside but Lee grabbed my arm and pulled me back so he could step in first. I elbowed him in the ribs as he squeezed past me, then followed. I closed the door.

Isaac went back to the couch and fell into the cushions; without taking his eyes off the TV he yelled, "Cable!" Gunfire arced across the screen and Asian men in tattered vests grimaced and threw up their arms as Rambo clenched his teeth and sprayed them with bullets.

"Yeah!" came Cable's muffled yell from down the dark hallway. I followed Lee and we walked as lightly as we could back to Cable's room.

Cable paused the game, his fighter frozen mid-punch. "You guys wanna play?" He offered Lee his controller and chair in front of the TV, and I hopped onto his bed.

Cable's room was also the weight room. Next to Cable's bed and TV stood a padded bench with rack and bar for a bench-press. Plastic-covered weight plates were strewn on the floor near a set of heavy-looking dumbbells. In the other corner was a brown dresser. A white sock hung from the top drawer.

"Wyland, how about you?" Cable asked.

Immediately my mouth tasted sour, my knee began to bounce, and my stomach tightened. This was the way I felt before a basketball game, or a cross-country race, or whenever

I walked into the Farmington Library and saw the shelves upon shelves of books—struck by a pang of nervous longing. I nodded.

Cable plugged in a second controller and handed it to me. He straddled the bench and leaned back against the wall with his hands behind his head, brushing against the cluster of medals that hung there, making them clink.

I went through the grid of fighters with the controller, the selection box clanging as it moved over each portrait. They were dressed in loose pants, belted kimonos. Some were shirtless and shiny. The women were thin and lithe with pointed breasts, clothes fitting tight to their bodies. Some fighters had cloth wrapped around their faces covering their noses and mouths. On the controller, the top two buttons for the right thumb were to punch high and low, the bottom two to kick. The cross on the left side of the controller moved the fighter forward and backward, while down and up made him crouch or jump. A good player like Cable could mix the buttons to make fire or lightning shoot from a fighter's hands, or a spike-tipped lasso spring from his palms to lodge into his opponent's throat. The thud of bone-on-meat sounded when punches landed, splashes of blood flew from their mouths.

"I don't know why he did it," Cable was saying. He was tapping the wall above his head beside the medals. "But you know Jake. He's crazy. This was the third time they caught him. Usually they just throw him out, but this time the boss called the cops."

I pretended I was barely listening. Lee was doing the same.

"Dad didn't even try to stop them."

I'd paused in the middle of choosing a fighter to make sure I heard every word. Usually Cable would've said "my dad," but he was almost talking to himself now. He wasn't a talker and I'd never seen him say this much without someone asking him a question. One summer Lee and I came back after being away on our uncle's farm in Idaho, and Cable had a scar over his right eye, like someone had been drawing his eyebrows and nicked his skin. I'd always suspected it was from a fight with his brother.

"Teach him a lesson, I guess," Cable said. "I've never seen Jake so mad. When he's mad he doesn't yell. He just gets quiet."

We waited but Cable didn't say anything else.

We had our fighters. I'd picked Liu Kang, a shirtless fighter with black pants and a red headband, while Lee had chosen Scorpion, the masked yellow-and-black ninja. The screen went dark before our first round.

"Dad said he was going to have to hitchhike home from Shiprock," Cable said. Shiprock was fifty miles away.

The screen came back up and the fighters were in a coliseum with screaming bloodthirsty spectators all around.

"Mom got mad at him."

Cable's mom Glenda was a kindergarten teacher and had taught both Lee and me. Like everyone, she adored Lee. Whenever we came over she gave us popsicles that turned our mouths purple, blue, green.

"She took the van to go get him," Cable said.

"Round one, fight!" commanded the game announcer in his deep voice.

Lee won the first round easily. Round two started. Lee began to kick my ass again. Blood sprayed from my fighter's mouth as Lee spun everything he had into a kick, then punched me into submission. I smashed the buttons, backing up as fast as my thumbs could press, trying to find some way to block. Lee closed with an uppercut that lifted me into the air and left me bloody and tangled on the ground. My fighter staggered to his feet like he was going to fight again, to make one last stand. But instead, he was helpless, hands at his sides, head rolling around his neck, swaying like he was drunk.

"Finish him!" ordered the voice.

Lee had his mouth open and was staring hard at the screen. He pressed a few buttons in succession—I heard each clack—and his yellow-masked fighter, released from his fists-up stance, walked over and ripped Liu Kang's skull and spine right out of his mouth. Scorpion turned to the crowd, held high the skull and dangling spine, while what had been Liu Kang collapsed into a pile of skin.

"*There* you go!" Cable said.

"Holy—" I said, and the music rose, hammering to a metal crescendo. The screen faded black.

"Don't worry, Wy," Cable laughed. "You're getting it." He had his hands clasped behind his head still, his biceps like potatoes. "Uppercut him," he said. "You need to learn how to throw that punch. It's the best move in the whole game. That and what Lee just did to you." He smiled, scrunching up his eyes.

We played some more. It felt like we'd only been playing for a few minutes, but when I looked down at my Casio, it was past noon. The sun was just starting to peek through the windows.

I thought I was getting the hang of it—hold the down button plus high punch to uppercut. But I still got caught swinging at air as Lee ducked, then smashed me into the ground.

"You going to join the basketball team this year?" Lee asked.

Cable lifted the twenty-five-pound plate and tossed it as easily as if it were a pizza. I'd lifted a blue one once, tried to spin it like Cable did, his hands thick and strong like Isaac's, and instead dropped it, smashing my index finger with all ten pounds. My fingernail turned black and at school I'd had to curl my hand around my pencil like a claw.

"We could use you, man. We need some guys who can play defense and rebound. We mostly have a bunch a skinny guys who just want to shoot." Lee looked at me. "We need some muscle."

I jumped over Lee and threw a fireball at his chest, and then as many more as I could punch in.

"Yeah, maybe I'll play this year," Cable said, lacing his fingers behind his head and leaning against the wall again. The sound of the front door slamming reverberated through the house. Cable raised his eyebrows like he was trying to look over his shoulders through the wall. When we didn't hear anything else, he continued.

"Riggs will be mad, though. He talked to me before school let out and said he wanted me to wrestle this year. He said I have lots of talent. Maybe even more than Jake." He tried to say it casually but when I looked over he was smiling and puffing out his chest.

I was burning through the characters like a slot machine, trying every fighter—blue Sub-Zero, shirtless Johnny Cage, and the rest—to see which one had the best luck, but Lee kept kicking my ass with Scorpion.

"Go ahead, try them all," Lee said. "Try the chick, you haven't tried the chick yet." I finally won a match with Raiden who shot lightning from his fingertips and wore a triangular hat I'd seen on Vietnamese farmers in a textbook.

"That's it," Cable said. "Get him with that uppercut."

"Don't give him tips," said Lee, but Cable just laughed.

We heard the back door open and then slam shut, felt it through the floor, too. We went quiet for a bit, waiting for Isaac to shout something from the living room about keeping it down. But he wasn't there. Then we heard heavy footsteps from the back.

"Hey, kids," Jake said. He was standing in the doorway. He wore a plain black T-shirt, baggy on his ropy frame. Black lace-up boots. He leaned against the doorframe, his long hands dangling. "Mortal Kombat, huh?" he said. "Who's the best here?"

We didn't say anything.

Jake looked at Cable, then me, and finally Lee. The game soundtrack played in the background, clanging, drumming, whooshing.

"Hand me that controller, Wyland." Jake nodded his head at me and held out his hand. "I know how this guy plays." Jake had grown into his body and his wiry muscles. His Adam's apple stood out from his neck like a rock stuck in his throat.

Sprinkled here and there over his head, visible through his buzzed hair were little scars, nicks like he'd laid down in a bed of glass.

But I'd just beaten Lee for the first time and I wanted to keep playing. The controller was made of smooth plastic. I felt the seam where the two halves came together, ran my thumb over the buttons, concave for punch, convex for kick.

Jake snapped his fingers at me. Raiden raised his arms to the sky, lightning shot from his hands straight up and off the flickering screen. Jake motioned again. I handed him the controller.

Jake pulled up the chair that had been lying on its side. "Now," he said, turning to the screen, "let's see." He flipped through characters and the blinking selection box paused at each portrait with a clang until Jake settled on the same black and yellow fighter as Lee.

"See," Jake said, "there's all these fighters but only one can win. Right, Lee?"

Jake pressed the buttons carefully, didn't smash them like me or rapid fire them like Lee. Blood splashed everywhere. But Lee beat him too, match after match, annihilating the twin fighter whose yellow outfit was just a shade darker than Lee's. Jake's shoulders twitched after a particularly good beating in which he hadn't landed one punch.

Then Jake laughed. He leaned back in the chair and smiled. "This isn't my game anyway." He stood up, put his hands on his hips, pushed them forward and leaned back, stretching like an old man. He looked around the room like it was the first time he'd been there. His room was down the hall.

Jake walked to the dresser and flicked the sock hanging from the top drawer. Then he put his hands on the dresser top and ran them along the edge like he was admiring the wood. "Check this out," he said and bent down and reached under the dresser where there was a small gap. We watched Jake's back as he fished around, then he turned his head and pressed his cheek against the bottom drawer to get a better reach. He went still for a moment. Then he slid something heavy out along the linoleum.

He sat back on his heels with his back to us, looking down at the thing in his lap. Without taking his hands off it he leaned back to one knee, got up easily and turned to us. The veins on Jake's forearm popped as he held the handgun out for us.

We didn't say anything.

"Oh," Jake said apologetically, "you can't see."

He took a few steps toward us, sideways so it wasn't pointing at any of us directly, but still we leaned back to be out of its line. The bluing on the barrel was starting to wear off, leaving gray steel underneath. I'd had a gun like this, that loaded through the bottom of the handle with a clip, too. But my gun was plastic, only shot caps, and had a big red stripe painted around the muzzle.

"Here, give it a try," Jake said, holding the gun out to Lee.

I could feel Lee tense up beside me, his back go straight. "Nah, man," he said. He still had the controller in his hand.

There was no beauty in that gun. It wasn't like our dad's Winchester lever-action with the brass chamber, not like the filigreed 12-gauge shotguns we blasted clay pigeons with in the summer, guns that punched our shoulders, leaving crosshatched bruises, guns that Grandpa oiled and cleaned like they were his children. We'd never used a handgun. Up close, the rim of the barrel was worn—it looked like it had been dropped, scraped along the ground, shoved into narrow places.

"Come on," Jake said, "it's just a piece of metal." He waved it at Lee, but Lee didn't take his hands off the controller.

"Ok then," said Jake, "I bet Wyland wants to try it, huh, Wyland?" He turned the gun toward me.

Lee reached for it, but Jake jerked the gun away and held it by his ear, pointed at the ceiling.

Jake held out his free hand like a stop sign. "Whoa!" he said, frowning dramatically. "Whoa there, Lee." He paused and his brow furrowed, and he looked at the ceiling as though he was thinking hard. Then he said, "I gave you your chance." He swung the gun down and pointed it at Lee.

Cable hadn't moved from his place against the wall since Jake stepped into the room. Now Cable moved and opened his mouth but only a funny whisper came out. He tried again. "Hey, man," he said hoarsely.

"It's okay, little brother," Jake said. Not taking his eyes off Lee, he motioned to Cable to stay where he was. "You know why they put me in juvie?" Jake said. "I know you want to know."

We didn't answer.

"I kicked that cop's window out. He was gonna let me go. He was calling Dad on the radio. *Hey there, Isaac, got your boy out here. Stealing. Again . . . basketball cards! You believe that?* I was cuffed in the backseat with my hands behind my back, listening to them talk. And know what Dad said to that? *Scare him.* So I kicked out his back window. Both feet. Took three kicks. *Boom, boom, boom.* Then it went out easy, all one piece. It busted but it popped out all together like it was taped."

Jake shifted his feet and looked down at his boots. They were tall, black, and shiny. "It was these boots," Jake said. "These are my kicking boots."

Except for the glance at his boots, Jake hadn't taken his eyes off Lee the whole time he was talking.

Jake shook the gun slightly. "Just like this is my shooting hand." He turned his head but not his eyes to me. "Isn't that what they call it, Wy? Your 'shooting' hand?" He laughed a little. "I was never good at that basketball. Not like you guys. You guys are so *good.*" He smiled. "Wrestling—" he wagged the barrel of the gun again and rocked his shoulders a little, "—that's my thing. Look at all that stuff on the walls. You see that? Champion!" He shouted again, "*Champioooon!*"

This time he took his eyes off Lee and the gun came down to his side and he shook his head around and bounced on his toes. And he did look like a champion. Even as I was thinking I might crap myself, I saw the wild champion.

Lee moved to step away and suddenly, so quick I almost shouted, the gun was back pointed at Lee's chest.

"Whoa, buddy—" Jake said. Lee froze mid-step. He slowly raised his eyes, not to the barrel, or Jake's eyes, but somewhere *past* Jake, behind his head. I knew that look.

Jake pressed on, "—And where's Dad *now*?" he asked. "Where's Dad, Cable?"

Cable, his eyes on the gun, gave a slight shrug.

Jake smiled. "Mom and me saw him leaving the other way when we came in—going to the store!—that's what she guessed." Jake shook his head again. "Probably afraid of me," he laughed. "Man!" Jake said, sighting down his arm and the gun at Lee, "This thing makes you crazy."

Stop fooling around, I thought, *can't you see this is a real gun?* My throat was squeezed tight. Lee's neck was tensed. He still had the controller in his hand. He was looking past Jake. Lee got this way when he was about to go off, like the fights at school. He was going to do something stupid, and Jake was ready for him.

I stood up, held my breath, stepped over the cord to the controller still in Lee's hand, and walked in front of the gun. The barrel brushed my chest and stayed there.

Lee grabbed my arm in surprise.

Jake's eyebrows went up, but he didn't move the gun.

We stood like that, Lee behind me with his hand holding my right bicep.

The trailer grew hot. My stomach twisted in on itself. We had missed lunch. The game music and the swamp cooler were far away. Jake was no longer smiling—now he had a sad look in his eyes. Cable stepped over like he was going to do something, and Jake turned his head just enough that he took his eyes off the gun.

Lee pushed me to the side and with his other hand swung down at the gun, which exploded.

*

Far away I could hear a ringing, like someone was honking at me from one end of a tunnel. It was like someone stuffed cotton in my ears. I was on the floor. I checked my stomach, my chest, my neck, and then I raised my hands to feel my ears. My ears were still there. Lee had his hand across my chest and was trying to push me back down.

The gun lay in the middle of the floor. Jake was kneeling over Cable, punching him in the stomach, and Cable was trying to roll over onto his side, squeezing his eyes shut as though he was holding his breath underwater.

"What!—The!—Fuck!" Jake punctuated each word with a punch.

Finally he leaned back, panting, his face red. He had spit at the corners of his mouth. Cable lay there coughing and gasping, eyes still shut. Jake scooted back to the far wall and leaned against it; then bowed over, his legs straight out in front of him, he rested his hands in his lap, palms up. Seated, like he was a patient at a ceremony.

I pushed Lee's arm off so I could sit up. The smoke had the same sharp pleasing smell we got after a round of shooting clay pigeons. The gun lay on the floor, strangely lifeless. Holding his stomach, Cable crawled over and picked it up. He held the gun backwards, hand around the trigger guard, and crawled to the dresser. He reached down and slid it back under.

On the TV, the game had switched to the demo reel, the fighters flying at each other, feet and fists first, meeting in the air with a smash.

Wordlessly, Lee, Cable, and I looked for the bullet hole.

At first we couldn't find it. Cable ran his hands all over the floor like a blind man.

Finally I saw a tiny hole in the linoleum floor like someone had stabbed a pencil through it, right by the TV stand.

*

We heard the front door open and close, then footsteps in the kitchen and clinking that sounded like dishes being put away. The water ran for a while, then was turned off. The house got quiet.

"Hello?" said a woman's voice. "Isaac is that you?" Glenda sounded worried.

Footsteps came down the hall. "Oh, there you are," she said, standing in the doorway. She had on a white blouse and her hair was around her face in a perm. But she looked tired, and when I looked closer her hair was losing its curl and her back was wilted.

"What's that smell?" she asked, tilting her chin. "Jake," her voice rose, and her shoulders tensed. "What's that smell? Are you smoking again? How many times do I have to tell you!"

Jake stared down at his hands. The air felt thick. Nobody spoke.

After a while, Jake looked up, the smile back on his face. "I promise I'll stop, Mom," he said. "It's the last time." He pulled his knees up and rested his arms on them, his hands dangling. "We were just playing with our friends here. You know, me and Cable against Lee and Wy, just like we used to."

Glenda relaxed her shoulders with a sigh and made a tired smile. "Oh, you boys."

She turned to leave but stopped.

"What are you all doing on the floor?" she said, searching our faces, suddenly on guard. She focused on Cable. "Were you boys smoking too? These boys can't be smoking," she motioned at me and Lee.

"We weren't smoking Mom," Cable said.

"And where's your dad?"

Quiet again. It was almost too much. Somebody had to say something. I opened my mouth.

"At the store?" said Cable.

*

I sat there getting the feeling back in my hands. We heard a car pull up and Isaac's voice calling to Glenda, saying something about work, checking in on things, needing the truck keys. We heard him rev it and pull out of the drive. A little while later Cougar started up outside, his barking getting louder as he got close to the house. He must have been following someone along the fence.

The barking was so loud it was like he was inside with us. The hairs on the back of my neck stood up and I wanted more than anything to kick him in the head.

*

We stood in the doorway and said our "laters" like nothing had happened. I walked down the steps to wait for Lee. Cable closed the door behind him. Cougar streaked toward me and skidded to a stop at the fence, kicking dust and gravel through the links. He growled and bared his teeth. Then he went off, barking and snapping his jaws, shoulders bunching and saliva flying.

I bent down and picked up a big piece of the asphalt from where it had crumbled from the edge of the Pashlakais' parking space. Cougar watched me. I reached back, winding up the way I practiced on the diamond, dropping my hand down to my back foot and bringing my front knee up slow past my belt. Cougar stopped barking. As I came around with the rock I was surprised to hear him start on a whine, and my arm went loose, and I wasn't trying to hit him anymore. But my aim was still true, and the rock flew through the fence with a *tink* and smashed with a solid thud into Cougar's nose. Cougar yelped and scratched at the ground, shaking his head. He scrambled to the far wall where he cowered in the shade, pressing his butt down, flattening himself against the dirt, whining and rubbing his nose with his paws.

I turned and Lee was watching me. He shook his head slightly, almost so I couldn't see. And just like that I was sorry. My neck grew hot and I knew I was turning red. I couldn't stop it. The fear rolled into sadness and welled up in my throat, then my tongue and my eyes. My shoulders shook, tears rolled down my face and snot ran from my nose.

Lee came over and stood by me and put his hand on my shoulder. He rested it there and that was enough. It made me feel good.

I wiped my face and nose. I shook my head and tried to laugh but it came out a cough. It was getting toward evening. Wispy clouds had come in and the summer sun splashed the sky with orange and purple streaks.

"Hey, man," Lee said and gave me an awkward pat on the back. It sounded like he was going to say something encouraging.

I shrugged out of his second try.

"Let's go home," he said instead.

I cleared my throat. "Beat you," I said over my shoulder.

I felt Lee reach for me, but I was already running.

II

DERRIN KINYONIE

Jordan, Lee, and I were playing a game of king of the court and I was struggling to stay on. I hadn't won one game. It was a Friday afternoon in May, almost the end of the school year when track and baseball season were over, and the buses had taken everybody home for the day. I was watching behind the goal pole of the junior high court, which had better rims than the stiff double rims on the high school court, holding my ball at my side.

Jordan dribbled past Lee with a quick step, then, as Lee tried to recover, Jordan hopped into him with his shoulder, catching Lee right in the chest so he let out a *huh* and was knocked backwards, leaving the lane open for Jordan's easy bucket.

"Bam, son," Jordan said, grabbing the ball out of the net. "Next!"

Lee shook his head in frustration and admiration. Jordan had been perfecting that move ever since their freshman basketball season ended and now he was unleashing it on us. As a skinny eighth grader I bounced off Jordan like a dodge ball off a brick wall. I put my ball out of the way, steeled myself, and went out to meet Jordan. That's when Derrin Kinyonie appeared from behind the junior high building. He was bouncing his own ball, happy as can be, but it was clear he wanted to play with us.

Derrin Kinyonie had short, dark hair. He liked to play basketball. He ran in the *Just Move It* races all summer. He liked to joke around, paid attention, mostly, in class, got away with shooting paper footballs through the goalposts of someone's fingers when he could. Except he *wasn't* normal. All of us could see that, all of us knew that. For one, he'd been raised by his grandparents. Who his real parents were no one knew, or if they did, I never heard about it. Some people even said he was adopted. That question was harder to answer. He was light-skinned with a funny nose, and now in sixth grade he had braces. And although he had short, dark hair, he couldn't do that right either. It was short in the front, but long enough to brush his skinny shoulders in the back. A mullet, when that cut had gone out of style ten years ago, even on the rez. This was the new millennium after all and no one would be caught dead with a mullet, with tight jeans, with tight shirts, wearing shoes without a logo, with aviator eyeglasses, aviators with the smoky lenses least of all, the kinds that we saw in our mom's and dad's yearbooks, the ones from the seventies where guys had mullets and wore headbands and the girls wore their hair down long, silky, and shiny. We'd be laughed out of the gym if we wore any of that stuff nowadays. But somehow Derrin Kinyonie didn't get the message. He wore his jeans tight, he wore T-shirts that weren't baggy, he wore generic basketball shoes that had four stripes on the side—instead of three—that everyone knew were from Payless. He ran around bugging to play in our basketball games at recess and lunchtime, to play catch with our footballs. Only as a last resort did you let Derrin on your team, only when everyone else was taken. Because he would run around like a crazy man, dribbling with his head down, heaving the ball at the basket without any kind of grace or style, calling for the ball, yelling "I'm open, I'm open!" and clapping his hands for a pass, all the while that silly mullet flapping around behind him, making him look, somehow, like a duck. You have to understand. These were our *lives* he was messing with. This was style and cool. And if you had Derrin on your team there was no denying it, he came in and messed it all up.

And there was another thing, the worst thing. He had a lisp. This was junior high, and he lisped all over the place. In class, on the court, after school, everywhere.

I was an eighth grader now, and we were the kings of junior high. My brother had been promoted to high school the year before, along with all of his friends and classmates, the ones who had been in our way last year—stars on the basketball team, football team, cross country team, the fine girls we stared after in the hallways, at recess, who we tried to impress at games, on the court, or by making jokes in Ms. O'Hara's language arts class, in Mr. Long's history class, by passing notes behind Mr. Whitehair's back as he made lame jokes in Navajo Language class, or on field trips to Skate America in Farmington. Now *we* were the eighth graders trying to impress our own girls, especially now that it was spring, April behind us, the winds dying down and summer about ready to burn through the clouds. We could smell the end of the school year rolling toward us when we would go our separate ways for the summer and not see each other again for three whole months and then we'd be freshmen in *high school.* This meant our teasing and flirting had expanded to after school, to sports practices when we'd see the girls running around the softball field, when we'd run with them on the dirt track, where we lingered as the activity buses circled the blacktop out front to take them home, to get one more laugh, one more smile, one more glance even.

Derrin had been on my cross-country team that year in the fall. I was the captain along with my best friend Roland. When we were away from school at meets, in Bloomfield, Teece, Rock Point, or wherever, it was both easier and harder to pick on him. Easier because I was running the team and I could pretty much do what I wanted. Harder because there wasn't any audience to see what kind of jokes I pulled. My sister Jess was on the team that year, too, before she went to volleyball full time, and Derrin was in her grade. Jess looked at me accusingly when I made jokes on him, like I was being a jerk. On a bus ride to a meet, Roland jammed half a banana in Derrin's ear and it was so funny I peeled mine and was about to do the other ear when Jess turned around in her seat and shouted "Hey!" and put a stop to it.

Derrin wasn't fast, but he tried hard, and he was always eager, always there, never missed practices. Unlike Roland, who was faster than Derrin naturally (our number two runner after me) but who was always jetting off to powwows to dance, or trips to Salt Lake or Denver with his cousins, or sometimes just skipping to hang out with Valencia and kiss and hold hands or something. He always seemed to want to be somewhere else, did Roland, to be somewhere better. But he was my best friend, and I couldn't say anything. And really I was jealous he got to go all those places and hang with the girls. I was afraid of girls. Terrified and fascinated by them, too.

I had run into Melissa Tso that winter playing basketball in the gym after lunch one time. The gym was always packed with traffic, people throwing the football up and down the length of the court, girls and big Sam Denison bumping the volleyball behind the bleachers, and at least three different full-court games of basketball going simultaneously on the one court. So it was no wonder I went up for a layup on a fast break, and while craning my neck to watch the ball roll off the rim, ran into someone under the goal. My outstretched hand, palm out, went right into Melissa's chest. Except it wasn't really a chest like I'd known, flat and bony like mine, or chubby like Tobias "Booty" Blackgoat's who loved to snack. No, Melissa's chest was soft, but also firm, kind of like a memory foam pillow that Roland had brought on the bus to one of our meets. I froze and my guts went liquid. Melissa gave me a funny look, then batted my hand away and pushed past me, getting back into the fray.

For the rest of the day I couldn't get my mind off what I had felt, not in History, not in Science—it stuck with me. It felt like the world had opened up, but whether like a book or a chasm it was hard to say. They weren't just girls anymore.

So when Derrin came up bouncing his ball, smiling and happy like usual, saying "Hey guys," but it coming out, "Hey guyth" you knew it was going to get real.

Jordan, buzzed short hair, solid and strong, taller than the average player but not as tall as Lee, was busy practicing his free throws. Jordan had been our star in junior high last year, had been the star on JV this year, and could smell varsity stardom next year. He pounded the ball into the pavement and adjusted his feet with each pound. *Blam, blam, blam,* all the time keeping his eyes focused on the rim. He shot, followed through, the ball arced in the warm air, the seams blurring in perfect backspin. *Swish.* I caught the ball from the net and passed it back to him.

"Hey guyth," Derrin said again. "Whatsup?" Except it sounded like "Whatthup?"

Lee looked at Derrin sideways, not wanting to say anything or encourage him. I didn't say anything either.

Jordan started his routine again at the line. *Blam, blam, blam,* shifting on the balls of his feet.

"Come on, guyth," Derrin said, just as Jordan was releasing the ball. Clang. The ball caromed off the side rim.

"Come on, guyth," Jordan said.

I grabbed the rebound. Lee sniggered. Jordan was a good mimic, and had used that skill to good effect this year mocking the teachers—I heard all about it every time I tagged along with them after school on Fridays and weekends. But Jordan was quiet in class. Off the basketball court, Jordan wasn't the most outgoing guy himself.

Derrin tried to spin the ball on his finger. It rolled off.

Jordan laughed.

"Just watch," Derrin said and tried again. This time when he spun the ball, it landed on his index finger, wobbled for a second, then he spun it furiously with his free hand, like the globe in Mr. Hansen's office, and the ball stayed upright this time, the orange rubber seeming to brighten. He let it spin for a while.

"Damn," he said. "*Syih*, huh?" he said, using the Navajo word for "cool," giving it emphasis. Somehow this "S" came out more S-like than any other S-word he'd said. He caught the ball and smiled. "You try."

Jordan snorted.

"Come on, Jordan," Derrin said again. "You try."

Jordan tried it. He spun the ball on his finger, caught it there and kept spinning. He went from his index finger to his middle finger, kept spinning it when it wobbled, looking through his finger at Derrin.

"Dang, pretty good," said Derrin, not taking the bait, in fact showing no sign that he understood. Jordan tossed the ball off his finger, caught it and faked a pass to Derrin, who, still smiling, jerked his head to the side. Jordan smirked, turned, and shot a long jumper. *Swish.*

"Wow, you're good," Derrin said. "Come on, let's play."

"We're already playing king of the court," I said.

"King of the court? Cool, what's that?" said Derrin.

I started to explain, but Jordan cut me off. "Check ball," he said and threw the ball at me. I threw the ball back at him and got down to play D.

At the line we'd drawn in chalk to represent the top of the three-point line, Jordan held the ball at his waist and pivoted his right foot back, away from me. I moved up a little, wary of his drive, but Jordan could shoot it from deep, too, and that was in fact where he made his living during games, how he was making his stardom. Jordan lifted the ball over his head and brought it behind one ear as I came up under him, my left hand out at his waist, left foot up, trying to make him drive left. With the ball behind his head he looked down—not at me exactly, but at my feet, my legs, staring intently, almost not even seeing me, but just seeing the obstacle of me, the equation of me. I was aware of Lee and Derrin watching us. I tensed up my abs.

Jordan brought his right foot up with a quick step, and brought the ball down with it. I stepped backward quickly to stop the drive, not wanting to get beat like Lee. I was back on my heels when Jordan went up for a wide open three-pointer. Helpless, I watched the ball sail overhead. *Swish.* He hadn't taken one dribble.

"Next," Jordan said.

"Daaamn," said Derrin, grinning and showing his braces. There was pure enjoyment on his face. "My turn, my turn." I'd been the star on the junior high team that year, but I was no match for Jordan. Derrin hadn't even made the team.

Jordan clucked his tongue. "Get out of here, man. Let's go, Lee." Lee grabbed the ball out of my hands and scampered onto the court, as much as the tallest freshman in school could scamper. "I got you," he said.

But Derrin had stepped up. He'd put his ball down on the side of the court.

"No, *I* got you," Derrin said, getting down in front of Jordan in a defensive stance. He looked ridiculous, bent low, hands out at his sides like the old-school coaches showed us at summer basketball camp, stiff (not coiled), his chest out too far, a breeze ruffling the mullet tail off his skinny neck.

"God damn," Jordan said and turned away to hide his laugh. "I can't do it, I can't do it, man," he said to Lee, who'd stepped to the side when Derrin came up.

"Get out of here, Derrin," Lee said and bumped Derrin, sending him stumbling.

"Hey, hey," Derrin said, still smiling. "Watch it, man. I'm *standing* here, bro." He said it half serious, but still joking. Derrin made an attempt to slap the ball away from Lee, but Lee pulled the ball away.

Smiling, Lee put the ball in front of him and said, "Try it."

Derrin tried to slap the ball away again, but Lee was squeezing it hard in his big hands, and Derrin's slaps did nothing to dislodge it.

"Move, man." Jordan said.

Lee shooed Derrin away, then gave the ball to Jordan and got down in a stance. "Alright, let's go." He stuck out his lips in concentration and eyed the ball in Jordan's hands. Derrin watched them from a few steps away. I watched from under the basket, leaning against the pole.

Lee covered Jordan's first two moves with quick feet and a strong chest, forcing him left, then Jordan picked up his dribble on the left block. Lee thought he had him. Jordan upfaked him and Lee bit, jumping to block the shot, leaving a lane to the right. Jordan stepped in for the easy two.

It was a beautiful play, showing both Lee's eagerness, strength, and athleticism, but also Jordan's canny patience and deception. On the basketball court they were shining examples of who we were, our aspirations, our promise—and our people rewarded them every winter with cheers and admiration.

"Good shot, Jordan!" Derrin cheered. "Damn!" He mimicked Jordan's move with an imaginary ball—shot fake and then stepping through for the shot. He would never be that graceful.

I withheld my praise. It would be giving in to Jordan's superiority to admit it.

"Next," Jordan said, looking at me. I could tell he was feeling confident by the way he flipped the ball to me. He would be especially hard to stop. Derrin darted in front of me and slapped the ball from my hands.

"Oh, stolen!" Derrin shouted and raced with the ball to the other end of the court—never looking up from his dribble—where he finally looked at the goal and went in for the layup.

But Jordan had tracked him all the way down to the other end, and just as Derrin went up, Jordan leapt and swatted the ball down hard as it left Derrin's hands. It flew off the court, bounced into the dirt, then began to roll down the hill and into the weeds.

Jordan kept right on running after the ball and Derrin, after recovering from his initial shock, said "Hey!" and ran after it, too. Lee and I watched from the other end of the court, laughing. Jordan came running back with the ball, Derrin on his tail. When they got to the cement court, Jordan dribbled, leaving the ball out tantalizingly to his side, daring Derrin to take it. Derrin, eyes big, swiped at the ball but Jordan whipped it behind his back, and went in for his own layup back at our side of the court. Lee grabbed the ball from the net and kept the ball out of Derrin's reach.

"Come on, guyth," Derrin said, the whine in his voice and his pleading eyes showing for the first time signs of defeat. "Let me play with you. We can play a game, a team game. Two-on-two."

The evening was half done. The days had been getting longer, the evenings stretched on. Off in the distance was Mr. Hansen the history teacher, doing his evening walk. He liked to walk briskly, and always with a long walking stick. He was bald and red-faced, the sponsor of the junior high student council. In the gym at recess once he'd been watching us play and called for the ball. Surprised, I passed it to him. He shot a long three pointer with a smooth lefty stroke. "It's there!" he said as it arced to the rim. It missed, but we could tell he had been a player.

Mr. Hansen waved in our direction from across the lot where the buses circled every morning to let the students off, and then every afternoon to pick them up to drive them to all the homes, all the houses at the end of dirt roads in Red Mesa, Dennehotso, Sweet Water, Mexican Water, Round Rock, White Mesa, Montezuma Creek.

"Hello, boys!" Mr. Hansen called out. He liked to think he was the "cool" teacher.

We all looked up. "Hey," called out Lee and Jordan in their cool, deepened voices. I waved back, suddenly conscious of being too eager.

"Hey, Mr. Hansen!" Derrin shouted and waved back jubilantly.

"Hey, Mr. Hanthen!" Jordan mimicked under his breath.

"Having a good game?" Mr. Hansen asked.

"Yeah!" Derrin shouted back. "I'm schooling these guys!" The lisp again. I could feel Lee cringe next to me.

"Okay, you keep at it!" Mr. Hansen said, raising his fist with the walking stick. You could tell by the way he gave his encouragement, freely and easily, that he knew that would never happen. We watched him turn and stride on toward the gate to the school campus, back toward the teacher housing.

"All right," Derrin said, turning back to us. "Let's play."

"Nope," Jordan said. "Go practice."

"T'áá shoodí," Derrin said, using the phrase for "please."

"You're not good enough," Lee said.

"Bullcrap, I *am* good enough," Derrin said. "I'm better than all those other sixth-graders, huh, Wyland!" He looked at me earnestly, his lisp coming out again.

I shook my head no and looked at him skeptically.

"Yes I am!" Derrin said. "Come on, just let me show you."

"Isn't it time for you to go home?" Jordan said. "Why didn't you catch the bus?"

"Two-on-two. Me and Wyland versus you guys."

"Go home," Jordan said.

"What?" I said. No way I was playing with Derrin on my team against them.

"Sorry, buddy, not today," Lee said.

Derrin looked down and kicked a pebble across the pavement. "Ah, you guys, you're not even good anyways."

"What?" Jordan said.

"You're not even good I said."

Lee and Jordan laughed. Jordan covered his mouth with his fist in the way they laughed in high school.

"Yeah, you're just a bunch of łíí' chogiis."

Lee stopped laughing abruptly. "What did you say?" he said, and there was an edge in his voice.

"I said you're a bunch of łíí' chogiis." The sides of Derrin's mouth went up in a grin. "You know what that means?"

I should say now that one of the other things that made Derrin different was he could speak Navajo fluently. This scrawny, lisping, light-skinned boy could speak Navajo as though it was his first language, because it was. He'd grown up with his grandparents, two solid Navajo people who believed in the clanship system and family and were standup people in the community. His short grandpa with the thick glasses and short haircut always said "Hello, boys" to us when we saw him on campus. He did something for administration, special services for the special-ed students, many of whom were most comfortable in Navajo. He could translate for them, try to put the lessons in terms they would understand. He was a little old-fashioned, with his creased slacks, simple black shoes, and polo shirts. I'd never seen much of Derrin's grandma. She didn't work at the school, but I'd have guessed she was the same. Before we transferred to Red Mesa, my brother and sister and I had gone to school for a while at Rock Point, where they taught half the day in Navajo, so we'd learned a bit of the language. But I wasn't fluent, and it gnawed at me when I couldn't say something I wanted to, when I couldn't communicate my most basic thoughts in class, couldn't write a simple paragraph saying what I'd done over the weekend. I looked with envy at my friends who could speak Navajo, who had access to a whole other world, who could understand what their grandpa or grandma was saying, who could understand the medicine man in the hogan when he gave them directions, who could share jokes with their friends that only they could laugh at. But I knew enough to know how much I didn't know. So I knew that Derrin had called us a bunch of castrated horses, horses with no balls.

"Łíí' chogii."

Lee's grin hardened. "Ha," he laughed mirthlessly.

Jordan kept laughing. The name-calling didn't seem to have the same effect on him—he didn't understand.

Even though the people cheered them and the girls screamed their names, there was always the undercurrent of jealousy, too. You couldn't walk around the high school like a big star, especially if you were just a freshman. Even now I understood this. One day I was flowing up through traffic on the outdoor court when I ran into what felt like a tree. I crashed to the pavement and lost the ball. My head was still vibrating as I got up, disoriented. My lip was bleeding where my teeth had cut into it. Leland Nabahie and his boys were pointing at me and laughing and I realized it was his lowered shoulder that I'd run into. Leland was good but he had never tried out for the team. The way he wore his jeans low, his hair slicked back hard, his smile sideways, his initials tattooed onto his knuckles, said he would never participate in organized teams. This was just one of the types that Lee and Jordan were running into there in high school, but they weren't the worst ones. It was the parents at the games, some auntie, some cousin who disliked your success and spread her poison to her relatives, the staff, and when they picked their fights with you, those were the ones to watch out for, who could hurt you.

"I know," Lee said, eyes bright, like he'd just had an idea. "We'll let you play with us if you can pass the test."

Jordan and I looked at each other.

"Pass the test?" Derrin said. "What test?"

"The test that everybody has to pass to play with us," Lee said.

"Want me to shoot a three?" Derrin asked. "I'll shoot a three. I'll shoot a three from half court." He started off toward half court, which was a long perpendicular crack in the cement court.

"No, not a three," Lee said.

He strode over toward where I stood by the pole.

"Come here," Lee said to Derrin.

"What? Why?"

Lee held out his hand in front of the pole, palm facing out, and looked at Derrin at the top of the key. He waved his hand up and down along the pole. "To play with us you have to punch my hand."

Derrin grinned and looked at us. After a moment's pause, he said, "No, huh-uh." His smile was both unsure and full of awe, as if being let in on some strange secret.

"Yep," Lee said.

Jordan stepped over. "Yeah that's what we make everyone do if they want to play with us." He looked at me. "Right, Wyland?"

I hesitated for just a second, then said, "Yeah."

"Nooo," Derrin said, drawing it out, half-smiling, still that mix of skepticism and wonder, waiting for someone to break.

"Come on," Lee said, motioning Derrin closer with his left hand. He was still waving his right hand up and down in front of the pole. The ball was on the ground off to the side of his feet, forgotten.

Derrin stepped closer carefully, glancing at all of our faces in turn. A chill went up my back.

"You gotta hit my hand right in the palm," Lee said. "Right in the middle." He'd made his face serious. "I know it's hard, but you gotta do it. It takes skill and timing. Just like basketball."

Jordan, standing just behind Derrin, smiled at this.

Derrin stepped in front of Lee. I stepped to the side to watch.

Derrin smiled unsurely. "That looks tough," he said.

"You only get one chance," Lee said. "So you gotta hit it hard. Right Wyland? You gotta hit it hard, right?"

"It's the only way," I said.

This seemed to convince Derrin. He set his feet. He slowly held up his fist, watching Lee's hand. Lee's hand was big. The hand went up and down, not fast, but not slow either—hypnotically, never stopping. Like a windshield wiper blade. The breeze ruffled the mullet on the back of Derrin's neck, the back of his neck that had a thin covering of small, fuzzy hairs.

Derrin opened his mouth and stuck his tongue against his top teeth in concentration.

"You can do it," Jordan said. "Hit it hard."

Derrin cocked his fist back even more, shifting his feet to get better position.

A crow cawed off in the distance. A gust of wind swayed the net above us. Lee's hand went up and down in front of the pole.

Derrin swung his fist as hard as he could.

PONG!

For a second there was nothing, no sounds but the ringing of the pole.

Then Derrin crumpled to the ground. He rolled on the ground, writhing, holding his hand. Finally he started screaming. "Ahh! ahh!" he screamed.

For a second Lee continued to wave his hand. Then he stood with his hand outstretched but still. We all stared dumbfounded at Derrin.

"Aahh! You athholes!" Derrin shouted, his face contorted.

I'd heard something crunch when Derrin had hit the pole.

He held his right hand close to his chest as he lay curled around it, writhing like he was struggling against a straight jacket, against hands that wanted to hold him still.

"Oh, shit," said Jordan. "He hit it."

Lee had a look of disbelief on his face.

"Whoa," I said.

"Are you okay?" Jordan asked. "Are you okay, dude?"

"I didn't think he was—" Lee said. He looked at me imploringly and let out a nervous laugh.

I knelt down next to Derrin. He was thrashing around. I didn't know what to do. I tapped his shoulder.

He pulled away like my touch burned him. "Fuck you, you athholes!"

I could see now that he was crying. Crying was the ultimate. You couldn't cry. You just couldn't.

Tears streamed down Derrin's face. He took in a deep, hiccupping breath, held it for a second, and then let out an airy wail. It was the sound of a helpless animal, and it took me right back to all the times I had cried like that, chased down and bitten by dogs, beaten by my brother, or ran headlong into a truck's bumper in a game of tag. When the world seemed cold and uncaring. How could it be this way? That was perhaps the most hurtful thing of all—that it didn't make any sense.

I backed off.

Jordan stood over Derrin. "Let me see it. Let me see it, man."

Derrin shook his head and continued to roll on the concrete.

"Let me see!" Jordan shouted.

Derrin looked up at him through his tears and slowed his crying. Carefully, gingerly, he pulled his left arm away from his right arm. We all leaned in. Derrin's right hand was red, so red, it seemed like he was wearing a strange glove. And it was swollen. It seemed to be swelling before our very eyes. The knuckles were already bulbous, the knuckle lines disappearing in flesh and whatever blood and liquid was gathering under the skin. But it was his wrist that was the worst. It had jumped sideways out of alignment with the rest of his arm, and what was clearly bone strained against his skin.

"Damn," Jordan said. "That's broken."

"Hey, man," Lee said, leaning over. "I'm sorry—" He was finding it hard to look directly at Derrin.

"Hey!" someone said behind us and we froze. We had been so focused on Derrin that we hadn't been watching out.

We turned. It was Mr. Kinyonie. "What are you boys doing?"

We didn't say anything. You could tell by his voice he knew something strange was going on.

"Who's—" Mr. Kinyonie said, looking down at the boy we were crowded around on the ground. The color seemed to drain from his face and his eyes went wide behind his thick glasses. "Derrin?"

Derrin's crying was quiet again. Just the quiet intake of breath, let out in breathy sobs. Looking down into his open mouth, I could see the shiny fillings in his molars, and they seemed to glint and ring metallically with his sobs. The shame had come with his grandfather here, but he couldn't stop himself.

"What have you done?" Mr. Kinyonie shouted, looking at us, his expression becoming angry. He knelt down next to Derrin.

"We didn't do anything," Jordan said, shrugging his shoulders. "He did it to himself."

Mr. Kinyonie tried to touch Derrin's hand, but he whimpered and pulled it away. Mr. Kinyonie breathed out through his nose impatiently and said sternly, "Let me see it!" Derrin offered up his hand resignedly. Mr. Kinyonie breathed in sharply.

"Goddammit!" He shouted, and I stepped back.

"Now we're going to have to go to the hospital. What were you boys doing?"

None of us said anything. Lee looked down at his shoes.

"What were you doing with these boys?" Mr. Kinyonie said to Derrin. "Sit up, son!" Derrin struggled with his good hand to sit up. "What were you doing with these boys?"

"We—" Derrin started shakily. "We were just playing basketball."

"Basketball!" Mr. Kinyonie said. "Bah!" He said it like that was all he needed to say, that the stupidity was self-evident. "Didn't I tell you not to play with high-schoolers? They just do this to you all the time."

Jordan sniggered.

Mr. Kinyonie turned to him. "What are you laughing about?" Jordan was nearly a foot taller than Mr. Kinyonie, but Mr. Kinyonie had thick, dark brown forearms and looked fierce with his eyebrows clenched in anger.

"Stupid boys," he said. "All of you. Yáadilá." It was a word for rebuke. He turned to Lee and I standing next to each other. "And you boys, I know your dad. You should know better." He shook his head disgustedly. "Picking on him. Don't you know he looks up to you?"

I hung my head.

"Hait'áo baantsídzíkeeso?" I knew he was saying something about thinking, what were we thinking? Somehow the Navajo hurt more than the English.

"Hait'áo baa . . . Doo ájít'íida!" he shouted at us.

I had heard that phrase of course, *It's not done*, plenty of times in school at Rock Point. And now, just like all those times, it made me feel small, squished down. Because it was also saying, *What kind of person does what you just did? How can you call yourself a person?*

Jordan wasn't feeling the same thing. But he knew the tone of voice, he'd been reprimanded plenty of times. "Psh," he said, shaking his head and turning away. "Man, whatever. I ain't got time for this." He motioned to Lee. "Let's go, Lee." He bent down and picked up the basketball and started walking toward the high school.

Lee hesitated. He looked at Derrin sitting up and cradling his arm on the cement. He wasn't crying as hard now, but he was moaning and sniffling and looking down at the ground, not wanting to meet anybody's eyes.

Lee made a gesture like he was going to pat Derrin's shoulder but he didn't touch him. "Sorry, man." He said. "Next time maybe. When that heals up." Then he went after Jordan, who was already bouncing the ball, heading toward the high school courts.

I was still standing there.

"Come on, get up, son," Mr. Kinyonie said to Derrin gruffly. He grabbed Derrin's bony left elbow and pulled him up.

"Ha!" Derrin yelped.

I could see now that it wasn't all unconditional love in their household, not like I might have imagined earlier. I'd never seen Mr. Kinyonie get mad, and it scared me, like it could go anywhere, and get anybody. Suddenly Mr. Kinyonie looked up and saw me there.

"What are you doing here? Go on! Go after your friends." It twanged a chord in me that he didn't automatically know who I was, didn't know my name like he knew Lee's. It happened a lot like that.

"Are you okay, Derrin?" I said, trying to find Derrin's eyes. But he kept his head down.

"What do *you* think?" he said and sniffled.

I went and grabbed his basketball from where it had rolled and held it out to him. "Here's your ball."

He looked up. "That's not my ball, that's *your* ball."

I looked down. Sure enough, it was my orange rubber ball, the pebbling worn almost smooth. Derrin hadn't brought a ball in the first place. He must have found mine on the ground when he came over and started playing with it. "You can have it," I said suddenly and held it out to him.

"I don't want it," he said, as if that was the stupidest idea he'd heard all day. He started walking with Mr. Kinyonie toward the administration parking lot across the way. I knew that hand must've been hurting him like hell but he limped like he'd hurt his leg. Eventually Mr. Kinyonie took his hand from Derrin's shoulder and walked by his side. I watched their backs, Mr. Kinyonie the same height as his grandson.

I couldn't see Lee or Jordan anymore; they had rounded the corner of the junior high buildings down the way. The sun was nearing the horizon and turning the sky orange. But we still had an hour of daylight. Just then I heard Jordan's bouncing basketball again. He stuck his head back around the corner of the building.

"Let's go, Wy!" Jordan shouted. "Get your ass over here, we're not done yet!"

I ran, dribbling the ball as I went, slowing here and there to throw in a move. When I remembered to look up, Derrin and Mr. Kinyonie were gone.

III

THE GLOAMING

It was one of those cool September mornings at my grandmother's house that meant summer was almost over. Dad and Lee worked on Grandma's old truck. We shot hoops with our cousins and played games of H-O-R-S-E and two-on-two on the goal bolted to the telephone pole. We played with the two dogs and the lamb my aunt was raising. She was keeping it in the house in a pen of cardboard boxes with an old blanket as its bed. We crowded around to watch her feed it. She sat on a chair, holding out the first of two milk bottles to the lamb, who opened its mouth and stuck its tongue out. "See," she said as the lamb greedily sucked down the milk. "He knows what to do." It wriggled its tail with happiness, scraping its little hooves on the plywood floor. "Here, you try," my aunt said.

We took turns feeding the lamb. It didn't seem to mind as the bottle changed hands. Its focus was on the nipple, my aunt said very matter-of-factly and I laughed. By the time it was my turn, the second bottle was almost empty and the lamb slurped out the last bit, then sucked the air bubbles until I pulled the bottle away. It tried to grab it again, but I kept the bottle just out of its reach. I played with its head and ears, knocking it around. Its ears were long and floppy.

"Gentle, gentle," my aunt said.

"Golly, it's not a dog, Wy!" said my cousin Missy.

We took the lamb outside and the dogs tried to play with it like it was one of them. The lamb tried to play too, but it was overmatched, and soon the dogs sent it tumbling, so we kept them apart. It bleated loudly and my aunt chuckled.

I had just started my sophomore year in high school where I had to keep my guard up, but at Grandma's I could just enjoy myself. I talked with Deidra and Missy about who Lee was going out with (even though he'd told me not to tell anyone), and about who I had a crush on (Leah George). My sister Jess challenged me to one-on-one and I tried my *And One Mixtape* moves on her, even bouncing the ball clean through her legs and going up for a layup before she pushed me in the back. I would have missed anyway—I was laughing too hard. Jess hated to lose.

When the sun had just passed midday Grandma stepped out in her flour-dusted apron and yelled, "Da'oosóo!" We dropped everything. She'd made a hearty lunch of frybread and hamburger sandwiches.

I was licking the grease off my fingers when the dogs started barking. I craned my neck from the table to see out the window: a red truck was bumping down the dirt drive.

"Who's that, Grandma?" Deidra asked.

Grandma just smiled.

As the truck came closer, I could see two figures, the smaller one in the passenger seat. The old man got out of the truck with the help of his cane. He already had his green headband tied above one ear and was wearing a turquoise necklace, concho belt, and everything. The medicine man. His helper, a man who looked a bit younger than my parents, grabbed his bag from the back and hurried to help the medicine man up to the front door.

All during the bustling, our hasty preparations, tidying the living room and heating food and coffee, my mother kept asking Grandma for an explanation. Just when she'd grown tired of asking, Grandma finally said gruffly, "For your protection!"

In the commotion Jess and Deidra tried to sneak off, but Grandma halted them with a sharp "Hey!" and made them come back inside.

Grandma instructed my aunt to lay down a few layers of calico material, folded just so, on the clearing we'd made in the middle of the floor, and the medicine man proceeded to take his things from his bag. He set down bundles wrapped in leather, a woven basket, arrowheads. We all went quiet, and the air grew thick. Us men sat on the south side of the living room, women on the north. The medicine man began to give instructions in Navajo, and Grandma directed us around, sending Auntie to find the gourd dipper to replace the metal one in the water bucket, Deidra for more pillows to sit on. And then we had a long sing, a prayer right there in the middle of the day in the middle of Grandma's living room. When the prayer started I strained to understand—I caught words and phrases that I knew that invoked holy things and places and beings, but the specifics of what the story was were lost on me.

By the time it was done—the tobacco smoked and the medicine man and his helper fed again—the sun coming in the windows had turned orange. Grandma was happy, brimming with accomplishment, and talked them right out the door and on their way to what sounded like another doing.

By then it was time for the rest of us to get in our cars and go home, too.

*

Dad was at the wheel of the minivan. Mom was still annoyed, the lightheartedness from the completion of the ceremony had worn off.

"She could've at least told us," she said to no one in particular. "What if we didn't want to pay for a medicine man? She spends so much money on them. Always pawning her jewelry."

"You know your mom," Dad said cheerfully. "Everyone was there. She wanted to get it done in one fell swoop."

"She could've warned us though," said Mom.

"It was great," Dad said. "Good for these guys. Right guys?"

Mom didn't say anything and instead looked sullenly out the window as we drove up into the sagebrush and snakeweed fields that led into Rock Point, still a half hour from home. We drove past the gas station, the school, and the post office, curved up onto the plateau for another ten miles, then turned right at Mexican Water for the last fifteen-mile stretch to home.

As we descended into the valley before climbing the last rise to home, we saw a big revival tent set up a mile off the highway, glowing. The big candy-striped tents always seemed so inviting standing out in a dusty clearing or bushy valley or plateau, glowing in the night, turnoffs marked by hand-painted signs.

"What do they do out there?" I asked.

Dad looked out, staring across Mom in the direction of the tent, and the van slowed down.

"Freddy," Mom gave Dad a sideways look. "What are you doing?"

Mom had an aunt who'd gone over to "the dark side," who pressed the bible on all her nieces and nephews. Anyone could tell how my mom felt about it. She said things like, "Why do they show the body at funerals? It's medieval." As I'd learned—paying attention the few times it came up because no one ever talked about it—traditionally you buried the body right away, and that part of the ceremony was done with the fewest people to limit your contact with whatever bad things were there. When it came to funerals Grandma always said, "They're children," and wouldn't let us go.

Dad slowed the van, turned on the blinker, and we turned off the highway onto a dirt road. We crossed the cattle guard with a buzz. Into the thick silence that had sprung up, Dad said, "The kids should learn about these things."

Lee, who was on the back seat beside me, woke up just then. "What?" he asked groggily. "Where are we?"

"We're home," I said.

"What? This isn't home." Lee shoved me against the armrest. Jess laughed.

Bushes scraped the bottom of the minivan. We parked at the end of one of the uneven rows of cars and trucks.

Mom shook her head and with her voice full of disapproval said, "What are we doing here, Freddy." But she got out anyway.

The air was dusty from all the cars. A big generator was hooked up to a diesel truck, its wires spreading out to the lights under the tent. The tent was enormous. The poles stretched the shiny, red and white-striped tent up so high it seemed like at its top the tent could've been taller than the roof of the school gym. Under the bright lights inside the tent were rows and rows of people sitting in folding chairs and a man was shouting at them. He was maybe fifty years old, Navajo. He was so loud his shiny gelled hair seemed to vibrate. He shook his fist, punctuating phrases that ended with "lord" and "sends down upon you." He held the crowd with his trembling energy and tremendous sound. He was like no one I'd ever seen.

The man ended his speech to loud applause. A band came out on the stage. I recognized Glen Shorty on guitar. He was a nerd at school who wore collared shirts every day and acted ridiculously formal with every teacher and adult, shaking their hands and things like that.

We had wandered to the edge of the tent, Dad and Lee in the lead. Mom had her arms folded. Jess stood next to me. I was very conscious of being out of place, of people starting to look at us. I stepped up and nudged Lee. "That's Glen, right?"

Lee ignored me, then without looking at me gave a curt nod.

"I didn't know he could play guitar," I said.

People clapped, raised their hands and shouted, "Bless us, Jesus!" And they *sang*.

After the song, Dad sat down in the back row where there were a few seats open. He motioned for us to follow.

"I'm going to wait in the car," Mom said.

"Oh—" Dad said, but Mom was already walking away. She tripped on an electrical cord and fell onto her knees. Dad made to help her up, but she waved him off angrily. She got up and stomped off.

"Okay," he said to her back, smiling sheepishly.

We sat down. Every minute of the next song I felt like eyes were on me. But I drank everything in—the band on stage bumping along, Glen strumming and moving his hands into exotic shapes on the neck of the guitar, bobbing his head, the people waving their hands, some with eyes closed. There was even a chubby old woman standing and *crying*. I'd never seen anything like this. We left at the end of the song.

Nobody said anything on the way back to the car. I concentrated on stepping carefully over the extension cords.

Mom was sitting in the passenger seat trying to read a book by the faint glow from the tent lights. I could tell she hadn't turned a page the whole time. We got in and Jess closed the sliding door—there was no way to do it without a good slam.

Finally, as we climbed onto the highway, Mom turned to Dad and said, "Did you get it?" Her voice trembled with barely contained anger. "Did you get your fill?"

"It was wonderful," Dad said, his voice light.

We watched them—we weren't about to say anything.

*

A year later, I carried a warm dish of scalloped potatoes with cheese crusting the top as we walked to a birthday potluck for Jake Pashlakai. It was a clear day in late August, that time when the daylight seems to stretch on endlessly, but finally the sun was sinking. It was Jess, Mom, Dad, and me. Lee was away at a summer school. The year before, Cable had gone to live with his aunt but I still thought of their place as Cable's house. When Cable was around we'd lived our nights on the neighborhood streets, playing basketball with glow-in-the-dark basketballs, football with battery-lit footballs, advancing down the street in fits and starts, using the trailers that lined the streets as down markers.

But this summer I was alone. Lee was in New Hampshire studying for the SATs to get a jump on college before his senior year. I'd sabotaged my own application to the summer academy, filling it out reluctantly after Mom's badgering, and when it was complete, I said I'd mailed it, but didn't. One, because I was scared, and two, because this time I didn't want to tag along in Lee's wake.

When we put him on the plane in Phoenix, I could tell he was relieved I wasn't going. He was happy, full of *bonhomie*, a word we'd learned from the SAT guide we'd been studying together. He was smiling, patting me on the shoulder in an uncharacteristic show of affection, telling me to be good and help Mom. Watching him wheel his big suitcase past the gate, then turn and wave, my spirits dropped like a rock. I couldn't imagine a summer without him.

*

The dinner was set up in the Pashlakai's yard. Already the main table was set with grilled hotdogs and hamburgers, three different bowls of potato salad, a stack of frybread, another of Navajo tortillas, and it looked like someone had brought a giant bucket of KFC from Shiprock. There was also watermelon, a green fruit salad, a pink fruit salad, an ice-berg salad with croutons, and a big pot of mutton stew with posole. To drink there were pitchers of red Kool-Aid, cases of Coke, Shasta grape soda, and bottles of RC and Pepsi. It was a feast.

I put our scalloped potatoes on the table, aware that the dish was at odds with the rest of the food, too fancy in our clear baking dish, and Mom took off the plastic wrap. Jess saw her friend Krista and went to say hi. I looked around for Cable, hoping he might've come back for this and I'd have someone to talk to. Roland lived down in the valley and I knew he wouldn't be here. I scanned the people, mainly people and families who lived on campus or worked at the school. There were teachers including Ron Stevenson, my favorite teacher with his giddy enthusiasm for science and chemistry, who was there with his white wife. There were security guards, cooks, administrators, and a number of people who I guessed were Cable's aunts, uncles, cousins, and relatives, but I didn't see Cable. More people were trickling through the gate. Jess had gone to sit with Krista. I sat at the table beside my parents.

I saw other people bowing their heads, so I bowed mine, too. Someone's uncle said a long prayer in Navajo and then Glenda, Cable's mom said, "Eat!"

Glenda bustled in and out of the house while we were eating, bringing out condiments, refilling pitchers of Kool-Aid.

"Eat up there, Wyland," she said to me. "You look like a stick. You've got a ways to go before you're as big as your brother. The girls like a boy with some muscle." She made her hand into a fist and flexed her arm. Then she gave me a slap on the back and I coughed out some stew.

"Oops," she said and massaged my neck and shoulders with painful squeezes. She was nervous.

More people were still showing up, and now all the chairs were taken at the tables and people had to sit on the ground or stand with their plates on the hoods of the Pashlakais' pickup or lean against the van parked in their driveway.

Glenda stood at the head of the food table with her hands together. "I want to thank you for coming," she said. "I'm glad to see you all. To have a dinner, you need people." She smiled. After a pause and a nod to the people at the gate, she went on. "Some of you have donated your food. Thank you. Some of you have donated sick leave for me."

She looked at Mr. Stevenson and then my dad. Dad nodded back to her.

"Some of you even helped us with money. Thank you."

Glenda paused, giving people a chance to drink from their cups and cans and wipe their mouths. She opened her mouth to speak again, then closed it. She smiled like it was hard to do and then her eyes went glassy.

"I want to thank my husband," she said. "He made this dinner possible with his work."

People looked around for him, and I realized Isaac Pashlakai's security truck wasn't parked out front like usual.

"I want to thank my son, Cable. Even though he's not here, I know he's thinking of us." She turned her head slightly, reached up and wiped under her eye with her forefinger. "And I know you came to see Jake, but he isn't feeling very well. He's very sick—" Her voice shook, and she paused. "And he can't see you right now," she finished with a wavering voice.

A dark car drove by slowly on the street, a bass beat rattling its panels, setting the windows on the Pashlakai's van buzzing, too. I caught snatches of Dr. Dre and Snoop Dogg out of the car's half-rolled windows.

It seemed like someone should go up there and help Glenda. Mom sat next to me, frozen with her hand on her mouth. Ms. O'Hara, the pretty, red-haired language arts teacher who lived one street over, looked down at the table and wiped the corner of her mouth with a napkin.

Glenda steadied herself with her hand on the table. It seemed like she was waiting for somebody, too. "If you haven't had any," she said finally, stopping to swallow, "there's ice cream for dessert. Chocolate cake is his favorite, but Basha's only had the white one." Then with a fierce smile she said, "We have chocolate ice cream, though!" Her cheeks caught the light. "And where's that Denis? Anyone seen Denis? I need to talk to him."

Denis's mom, Mrs. Mason, who lived just a few houses down the street, busied herself picking seeds out of a slice of watermelon.

The cake read, *Happy Birthday Son Brother & Friend Jake* in white cursive on blue frosting. There was a picture in icing of a gold medal that said *1st* and hung from a frosting strap.

On my way back from getting plates of cake for me and my parents I spotted Leah George. I dropped the plates off, mustering courage. Miraculously, there was an empty seat across from her at her table. Feeling my ears buzz, I took my cake and sat down across from Leah. She looked up and smiled.

I mumbled hello and took a bite of the cake. Leah giggled and told me that the cake had turned my teeth blue.

"By the way, where's your brother?" she asked. Leah was a rising senior like Lee. "I thought he'd be here," she said.

She was wearing a black blouse that clung to her sides and the low button front stretched across her breasts. I hid my teeth and tried not to look at them. I tried to say something but because I was still worried about my teeth it didn't really come out at all.

"What?" Leah said.

"East coast," I said finally when my mouth was clear.

While the rest of us had pimples, Leah somehow had smooth, light-complected skin. This was going to be their school to rule this year, to demand *fealty*, another good SAT word, from the rest of us underclassmen. They would be the ones whose voices we quieted for, whose insults could shred our standing or whose praise could lift us up. Leah's little sister who had braces was in my grade and she was always after me at dances. K-Ci & JoJo came on and she would be searching me out, giggling with her friends and covering her mouth.

Roland would snigger watching me try to be inconspicuous, inevitably pointing me out and waving them over.

"He's away at summer school," I said.

Her face fell and it was like I'd been kicked in the stomach.

"Somewhere in New Hampshire or Connecticut," I said, trying to recover my cool. Saying *New Hampshire* and *Connecticut* sounded smart, sophisticated. Lee had called home a couple days before and after Mom had talked to him she asked if I wanted to talk to Lee. I made a show of dragging myself to the phone. After a few awkward moments he said how he could hardly sleep because of the humidity and there was no AC in their old dorms. But he didn't sound frustrated or sad. He sounded upbeat and energized. I could hear someone, maybe his roommate, talking in the background, trying to ask him a question, boisterous, already fast friends with my brother. Not for the last time I regretted not going. Even if I'd been his sidekick, I'd still have been on the adventure.

"Such an overachiever that guy, right?" Leah said.

I laughed noncommittally.

I went for another slice of cake. Leah had politely declined. It struck me that the cake decoration was too childish for Jake, who had graduated the year before, somehow cobbling together enough credits, defying his delinquent reputation. Jake was a wrestler, a bully with a crooked smile who haunted my dreams, dropping stinkbugs down my pants so I woke to the smell of their acid stink coming off my own sweat. I'd heard from Mom that he'd stopped going outside, saying the sun bothered him. It was hard to square this with the image of Jake in my mind. His mom thought he was just being moody and unsure of what to do after high school. He complained of headaches. Then they'd found the tumor.

As I made my way back to sit with Leah, Cable's big cousin Jeremy stood up and started singing "Happy Birthday" deep and off-key. Soon everyone joined in. Dad, a table over, belted it out in his scratchy voice. My first "happy birthday" cracked in my throat like I was 13. I looked over at Leah and she was laughing at me, but not in a mean way. It was a bright sound and made me smile and my heart pound.

And many more! bounced off the walls and cars.

Then a hush fell, and I turned to look. Someone was standing in the doorway, framed by the glow from inside. He was holding the screen door open like he hadn't fully decided if he was coming out.

I almost didn't recognize him. He didn't look like the wrestler, the Jake who had kicked out a cop car's back window. He wore a black shirt that even buttoned up to the neck was too big and hung from him like he was a wire hanger. The porch light above him lit up his face. He wore dark sunglasses that hid his eyes, but under the left lens were strips of white tape that attached to his eyebrow, forehead and cheek. The glasses fit crooked because of the bandage. The doctors had cut out his eye to get inside.

Jake was defined by his meanness, his easy power over kids like me. He was in that way invincible in my mind, one of those people we'd never be rid of, one of the natural forces of the world that you didn't question. Jake just was. But this was a boy, the first time I'd ever thought of Jake as a boy, scared and frail. I'd never seen it like this, descending not upon an old grandmother or grandfather but on someone like me, who just months before had been young, strong, smooth-skinned.

"I just wanted to see what you all were shouting about," Jake said. His voice still carried. The sound of his own voice seemed to buoy him, and he grew more solid. He stood, relaxed and cool. This crowd was here for him, his crowd.

"Jake!" shouted a man with thick brown glasses. "Hey, Jake!"

People shouted, "Jake!" "It's Jake!" "Get over here, Jake!" "We knew you were hiding in there!"

Jake's wide cousin Jeremy went up to hug him on the porch. The contrast in their bodies made Jake look especially thin. Jake didn't move his own arms to hug back. But he was smiling, and even behind the sunglasses you could see an honest joy stretch across his gaunt face. The cousin stepped back and began to talk with Jake, and others seemed to take the cue, scuffing chairs in the dirt, making to get up, get in line and say hello.

But before they got far, the tall man with the brown glasses stepped up and abruptly shouldered Jeremy out of the way. Jeremy looked astonished at first, but then he seemed to recognize who it was and backed away off the porch steps.

The man with the glasses stood squarely facing Jake and smiled, then he put his hand on Jake's shoulder. Jake went stiff, like cold water had been poured down his back.

I noticed a slight chill in the air. The people around us shifted in their seats. Some sat up straighter, while others began scraping their paper plates of leftovers, making to get up and leave. I saw Jess standing with Krista at the fence, their conversation paused, their attention now turned to the front door.

The man in glasses stepped up to the top of the porch with Jake and turned to face us.

"This boy Jake has been through a lot," he said. His hair was pressed down on the sides of his head from the straw cowboy hat that he now held in his left hand. "My nephew Jake." He used the hat to gesture at Jake next to him. He spoke like someone accustomed to talking and being listened to. I couldn't tell if he was really Jake's uncle or if he just called a lot of people "nephew."

"I've known Jake for a long time, and he's always been a good boy, a good young man. He's had his trip-ups, sure, I'll be the first to say." He chuckled and looked at the ground. "That time with the superintendent's garden, you all remember that, that was a good one." He straightened back up and grew serious. "But he's always been a good boy and everyone can see that. The Lord can see that." He gestured upwards with his hat. "In times like these we can use His strength."

I couldn't see his eyes because of his thick, tinted glasses. The glasses were like a mirror maze in the way they made his eyes sink into his head. It seemed condescending for him to call Jake a boy.

"Yes, sir, the Lord works in the way they call *mystery*" he said, putting a dramatic emphasis on the last word, like he knew better. "But he always answers the ones who call for him. The ones who humble themselves and call for him. He answers every last prayer one way or the other." He smiled at us. "Isn't that right?"

The people muttered. Ron Stevenson looked over at his wife and nodded his head toward the gate. They got up,

Stevenson taking his wife's hand, and left. I looked at Mom, who was trying to catch Dad's eye, but he sat there fascinated, his elbow propped on the table and his fist pressed against his goatee, a look of rapt attention on his face.

"Fred," Mom hissed, but Dad wouldn't take his eyes away. "Dammit, Freddy!"

"—So we are here tonight for this boy. For this young man. For this Jake. For his strength and his salvation. The evils, the devils out there, have tried to take him from us, but like always we are here. We are here to bring him out of the darkness that has covered this family and lead him into the waiting arms of the *Lord*."

The man reached over and took off Jake's sunglasses. Jake dropped his head like he'd been struck and the yellow light shone off the back of his neck. He wouldn't look up. The man raised his hand with the sunglasses into the air.

"Help me now, brothers and sisters, in Jesus' name. . . ."

My mother stood up. "Fred, we're leaving." She reached over to my table and grabbed my arm.

"What if I want to stay?" I said. I could feel Leah watching.

"What if you want to stay?" my mother asked incredulously, smiling at me as though it took all her energy.

I didn't know if I did want to stay. But it was like a curtain was falling and I had to decide quick which side I was on.

The patch over Jake's eye stuck out from his face like they had simply plugged a hole. With his good eye he looked out at the crowd. He was scared. For the first time I felt sorry for him.

The people who hadn't left, and it seemed like more had come as it had gotten darker, gathered around the porch where

Jake stood and raised their hands to him. The Glasses Man took a step down so Jake was alone on the top step, and poured out his words, words about taking away shadows and ghosts. "In Jesus' name we call on you."

Other people started to join in. Mrs. Mason walked over with her hand up.

In the middle of this, Mr. Pashlakai finally showed up, looking like he hadn't slept in days, still wearing his security uniform, and while he didn't raise his hand, he stepped into the crowd, too, his head bowed. Glenda sat alone at the edge of the light away from the crowd and stared away from the scene into the park, her hair shining red and purple.

Mom swung her head around at all the people, the waving hands, cornered. She squeezed my arm until it hurt.

"Ow," I said.

"Fine," she said, and let go. She turned and walked away. I watched her go through the gate, leaving the glass pan with our barely-touched potatoes on the serving table. At the gate Mom reached out, put her arm around Jess and steered her roughly away from a startled Krista, who had been in the middle of a sentence.

The people's raised hands trembled like fish, flashing pale, then dark. A single stream of tears came from Jake's good eye, and he reached to wipe it away with his skinny arm.

I looked around again, suddenly missing Lee. He would have known what to do. He would have held his ground, shown his support somehow.

The Glasses Man raised his other hand with the hat so now he had both hands raised, reaching like he would find an edge and pull the sky down around us. "Let it go!" he shouted, and the people started to wail. They started to say things I couldn't understand—some strange language. Not English, not Navajo, but a babbling, blabbering sound, men yelling and women groaning. I was afraid. I looked around for Mom, but it was just me and Dad.

"Help us, Jesus! Save us! Let it all go!"

*

"Well," Dad said, blinking like he was just waking up. I'd left Leah's table to sit by him. She hadn't noticed. She still stared with fascination at the scene.

Dad and I, on the other hand, had seen too much. It was no longer an adventure. I picked up our glass pan still half full with potatoes and followed him out. At the gate I looked back. Jake was looking in our direction. I opened my mouth to say I don't know what. But we had never been friends. Too much time and space had come between us, like a river, like Glenda's silent crying among the hands.

*

Out in the street, Dad walked ahead, as if to reflect on things.

A little way down, Denis leaned against a car. It was the dark one that had cruised by before. He wore a T-shirt with a giant portrait of Tupac on the front, complete with a diamond stud in one nostril.

"What are they doing in there?" he asked me, gesturing with his chin.

"Praying," I said.

"Not that again." Denis said. He'd heard it all, I thought, and that was why he waited there, the Chevy humming, Dr. Dre still rapping but turned low.

I left Denis like that, waiting for his best friend to get better, to come out like everything was alright, to have a smoke, to go for a ride, and hustled with my potatoes to catch up with Dad.

*

When we got home we knew we had to walk softly, to not let the screen door bang, to take off our shoes, to say we were sorry.

Mom was at the kitchen sink, her back to us, rattling the dishes, scraping the plates into the sink, and I could tell from her hunched shoulders that her brow was furrowed in anger and worry. On the couch reading a magazine, Jess looked up at me but didn't say anything. It was a *told you so* look, mixed with envy that I'd got to stick around a little longer.

"We're home," Dad said.

Mom didn't look up from the dishes.

I took the heavy glass dish to the kitchen and placed it on the counter. "Here's our dish, Mom."

Mom took the dish and shook the potatoes into the trash bin, shaking the dish hard because the last few slices were stuck to the glass. She dropped the dish loudly on the counter, and the bang sent a jolt through me.

Then she took a deep breath. She turned to me and wrapped me in a hug.

She squeezed me for a long time. I could feel the water from her gloves soaking into my shirt. I let my hands hang at my sides. I remembered Jake when Jeremy bear-hugged him. I lifted my hands and touched Mom's back.

She pulled away, glassy-eyed, and said, "Thank you." Then she sniffed and turned back to scrubbing the dishes.

Afterward, Jess asked me what happened. I told her about the people and the wailing. She said she'd seen that.

"Then Denis showed up," I said.

Jess said she'd thought that was him. In the car creeping down the street. That he was sitting real low, trying to hide when they walked by.

*

A few months later, my mother and I went to visit the Pashlakais in their new home one street over from their old one. Jake was dying, and he lay bandaged in his back room. Mom sat with Glenda, held her hand as she cried and cried, a soft crying that only once leapt into a sob. Lee was away somewhere, on a school trip for the seniors. Mom looked at me and I went outside.

I was a junior in high school, thinking I was a man. I miss those days of teetering boyhood, the sweet smell of rain in the dry earth, running hard through a tackle, sprinting to the basket, picking goatheads out of the ball after it has rolled down the hill. *Just pick it up, Wy, we ain't got all day, the sun's going down.* Cable had moved to Chinle a year after the thing with us and Jake, to live with his aunt and uncle, to finish out high school.

Outside, someone was in the yard, sitting on a stump with his back to me, scratching lines in the dirt with a stick. He stood up when I came out. It was Cable. He had filled out, like I knew he would, and his hands were strong, knuckles already turning knobbly. But I had grown, too, and as I walked up to him I could see I was taller than him now.

"Damn," he said. "Look at you, Wy." In spite of everything his face broke open in a genuine smile. He had glasses now and they went up with his cheeks as he smiled. "Not a little kid anymore."

And I realized with a dull pang that he had seen me as a little boy back then. But I was used to that reaction now after so many uncles, aunts, great aunts, old friends who I hadn't seen in years had remarked on the newer, sharper angles in my face, my height as I had outstripped them, early manhood opening before me like a book. Even though we had never hugged I went to hug him, but Cable held out his hand. We shook, and in that moment acknowledged adulthood in each other.

We stood there for a bit not knowing what to say, just basking in each other's presence. Then like a bad dream bubbling up in the middle of the day I remembered Jake alone in the back room of the house and my smile went away.

"I'm sorry," I said, not knowing if it was for Jake, for Cable, our friendship or brotherhood or all of it.

"Yeah," Cable said, and he looked off into the distance, knowing what I meant. "It's alright."

A breeze ruffled his short hair.

"Still playing basketball?" he said.

I nodded.

He smiled again and tilted his face up, jutting his chin at me in a nod. "Star player, I bet."

I welled with pride and felt my face grow warm. When I could look at him again, I asked, "Still wrestling?"

"Nah," Cable said, and his smile turned wistful, knowing, like he was protecting me from something. "Had to finish school, man. Had to focus."